C000147399

About the Author

Dorothy Lockyer has been writing poetry throughout her life, through many different situations and circumstances, finding humour in some tough situations. She has a love for animals and nature and tries to provoke thought and appreciation in others through her verse. After being diagnosed and treated for cancer, she decided to seek publication for her work.
As a 'Thank you' to Macmillan Cancer Support for their care and kindness, Dorothy will donate a percentage from the book's revenue to them.

Dedication

Many people, family and friends have inspired and encouraged me,
taken the time to read through the poems and to give honest and
constructive criticism. Thank you all, I am very grateful.

Dorothy P. Lockyer

POTPOURRI OF POETRY

AUSTIN MACAULEY
PUBLISHERS LTD.

Copyright © Dorothy P. Lockyer (2016)

The right of Dorothy P. Lockyer to be identified as author of this work has been asserted by her in accordance with section 77 and 78 of the Copyright, Designs and Patents Act 1988.

All rights reserved. No part of this publication may be reproduced, stored in a retrieval system, or transmitted in any form or by any means, electronic, mechanical, photocopying, recording, or otherwise, without the prior permission of the publishers.

Any person who commits any unauthorized act in relation to this publication may be liable to criminal prosecution and civil claims for damages.

A CIP catalogue record for this title is available from the British Library.

ISBN 9781785548628 (Paperback)
ISBN 9781785548635 (Hardback)
ISBN 9781785548642 (eBook)

www.austinmacauley.com

First Published (2016)
Austin Macauley Publishers Ltd.
25 Canada Square
Canary Wharf
London
E14 5LQ

The Hopeless Navigator

It's holiday time, and a touring we go!
With written instructions and maps to follow,
You can't lose your way, or possibly go wrong
So just settle down as you poodle along.

The time ticks on past, the miles slip by
Enjoying the countryside with a contented sigh!
Fields of crops, villages with strange names
So many different sights your interest claims.

A voice breaks through your contented reverie,
Asking, "where are we now?" Oh dearie, dearie!
Your fingers have slipped, and the maps gone askew,
It might not be this page, fancy asking you!

Thank goodness now; we are on the right road
Tankers and lorries flashing by with their load,
Deliveries to make, ferries to board,
Burning petrol and derv that none can afford!

On reaching a roundabout, which road do we need?
Stop admiring the fields of rich yellow rape seed!
I think that's the one, yes, I'm sure it is.
Whoops! Wrong again, and we're in a right tizz!

This road unfortunately turns into a lane.
Nowhere to turn, and no, that's not my name!
A few choice words and a six point turn.
As you pick up the vibes, will she ever learn!

Back on the right road, we're up to speed
Reading all the road signs to see where they lead.
Tensions are rising, the blood pressure too!
Oh, I wish we could stop and visit the loo!

We've reached the camp site, oh, what a relief,
Arriving in tact, without coming to grief!
The kettle is on for a nice cup of tea.
Put the comfy seats out, just under that tree.

Off to the moors now to visit the train
So well signposted, with picture and name,
But alas the parking was a hopeless event,
No room for us, so off we went!

We find ourselves in a very narrow lane,
Just by a signal box, manned for the train.
We twist and turn, go back and forth,
Facing east then west, trying to go north!

You can imagine the scene, slightly tense!
No wonder we missed the crack, snap of the fence.
But the signal man heard it, saw it too,
And was there with his notebook, right on cue!

Name and address supplied on the double
A new fence for the railway; are we in trouble!
I think we'll find something different to do,
Just go on our journey and enjoy the view.

It's time to move on, get back on the road
With maps and instructions for a repeat episode!
But after a short while, it's evidently clear,
I have to own up, we shouldn't be here!

I confess without doubt, I know not east from west.
I am not a navigator, but I tried my best.
A sat nav or TomTom, the answer might be.
But I can confidently say, don't ever ask me!

A Victoria Plum

Last spring my very short life began
In an orchard where the little birds sang!
Delicate blossom; buzzing bees working away,
Pollinating in their inimitable way.

A Victoria plum tree, with branches spread wide,
A secret place for insects to hide.
Patiently waiting, as showers of rain,
Refreshed and sustained her again and again!

Then gradually I began to take shape.
Small and hard, about the size of a grape.
As time went by with the sun's gentle heat,
I ripened and softened, becoming juicy and sweet.

The farmer would come and inspect us each day.
"There be a good crop of plums" he'd say!
That would make us proud, our skins would shine.
Mine the colour of autumn, a shade of good wine!

What's happening? I'm being plucked from the tree.
A market's been mentioned, which means nothing to me!
I've been put in a box, shut away from the light,
Oh, where is my orchard so pleasant and bright?

That was a shock, but I'm now on display,
With all my mates, on this sort of tray.
We have a label and a price on our head.
But I'm feeling quite anxious, a sort of dread.

The market stall holder treated us well,
But something within me needed to quell;
As faces came close and fingers did poke;
For a Victoria plum, this isn't a joke!

I with my mates were put in a bag,
It nearly split my skin, I'm feeling that sad.
Who could have thought what would happen next,
As I was broken and bruised and totally vexed.

A knife was taken to my golden skin
My sob wasn't heard above the noise and din!
A stone removed. Hey! That was my heart.
Add sugar and spice, as they said I was tart!

What am I now? I'm labelled "Plum Jam"
But for all the trauma, I'm tasty, I am.
I forgive you Brian; for your treatment of me.
Don't let your conscience put you off your tea!

AGE

Tis a strange phenomenon I wish to convey,
As I look at my family, my friends and say,
Why is it you age and leave me behind?
I don't wish to be harsh or even unkind!

But, as in my teens, I still feel the same
Age has not touched my inner flame!

Who is that young man, so full of charm?
Could it be the babe I once held in my arm?
The toddler, the lad I nurtured while growing?
Have years flown by without my knowing?

But, as in my teens, I still feel the same
Age has not touched my inner flame!

Where is the man who was so debonair?
Is that him there with receding hair?
Eyes growing dim; gaps where teeth should be!
Help! I'm married to an OAP!

But, as in my teens, I still feel the same
Age has not touched my inner flame!

I look in the mirror at the start of the day
That's not me I see getting old and grey.
The image familiar, but too cloudy to see
As the face of my mother stares back at me.

But, as in my teens, I still feel the same
Age has not touched my inner flame!

Where is the pup with his inquisitive nose?
Eager for walks, not wanting to doze.
Chasing the squirrels, the cats and rabbits.
Now keeps his head down, ignoring those habits!

Perhaps like me, inside he's the same
Age has not touched his inner flame!

And you my friend, what is your view?
Do you see me, as I see you?
Forgetful; asking "what made me come here?"
Faculties failing, often acting right queer!

Are you in your teens, still feeling the same?
Age has not touched your inner flame!

Living and Dying

I am being formed, out of sight
It's warm, enclosed and very quiet.
Life blood pulsates through my form
Do I feel happy? Or perhaps forlorn?
Is there a purpose for my being here?
Perhaps in time life will become clear.

Did I die? No, I am very much alive
Expelled from comfort I yell and writhe.
Alone no more, there is contact and sound,
Freedom of movement, no longer bound.
Growth, development, hope and ambition.
Bubbles of laughter, tears of contrition.

There is belonging, encouragement, choice
Fantasy and reality, silence and a voice.
Rules and limits to keep one from harm
The elixir of life to prevent hurt and alarm.
There is truth, trust and contentment
A loving gift to the child from a parent.

Colour and light has been stripped away.
Confusion, pain, the world has turned grey!
A precious life abused and betrayed.
Deprived of childhood, sad and afraid.
Burdened now with secrets and shame,
Living will never be quite the same.

The years pass by with increasing speed
Faculty loss; which intrude and impede.
But deep inside in the core of one's being,
The secrets remain locked in, no freeing.
Throughout life, never really being true
For fear of revealing the fiend, that is you.

Life comes to an end. So what is dying?
Is it perhaps life's final refining?
Finally, the last intake of breath.
Death after life? Life after death?
Now hope and faith come into play,
Is there to come another day?

The Squirrel

I am a squirrel, and I'd like you to know
I'm sad and bewildered and feeling quite low.
Since the day I was abducted and put in a cage
Something a poor squirrel could never envisage!

Let me introduce myself, Squiffy's the name,
I was born in an oak tree, just up the lane.
Our drey was large, comfy and warm
The work of my parents, before I was born.

Twas the middle of March, a warm spring day
The crows, jays and magpies chatting away.
We entered this world, that's me and my brothers
Three of us together, there were no others!

Percy and Peg, that's my dad and mum,
Fed us and cleaned us, life was great fun!
They taught us to run along branches of trees
To be wary of people and large bumble bees!

We grew more adventurous as the days went by,
Our escapades told, our parents would sigh!
Life was exciting, but could be scary also
As we learnt who were friends and who the foe.

Now Sniffy and Spiffy, that's my brothers and me
Found an exquisite garden that was open and free!
There was food in abundance, just hanging there
We didn't wait to be told to take our share!

The other residents in the garden seemed pleased
When we visited them and played and teased.
Sometimes a bit shirty, when we ate their nuts
But there were fat-balls and seeds as well as nuts.

This garden was pleasant, with shrubs and a lawn;
In a paddock, two horses called Ryan and Storm.
We chatted to them, and oh how we giggled
At their antics to get their Masters niggled!

But alas these are just memories now
'Cause on an ordinary day, I know not how
I was in this garden, tucking into a nut
As I realised my plight, when the cage door was shut.

To a place called a forest, whisked away
No one to talk to, with no one to play.
How I miss Sniffy, Spiffy, Mum and Dad too.
The other creatures I meet, say, "we don't know you!"

My days are spent pining, and I often weep,
My appetite poor and I'm frightened to sleep.
It's getting harder each day to display my fine tail
Life really for me, is beyond the pale.

But memories linger, and perhaps one day
A nice female squirrel will come my way,
Be touched by my plight, take pity on me.
Become Mum and Dad and have our own family.

CANCER

The year twenty twelve; as Easter draws near
A time to reflect on the things held dear.
A time to seek answers to questions deep
A time to be strong, though feeling so weak.

Spring is awakening, daffodils wave,
Birds full of song, as for a mate they crave.
Fresh green leaves bursting open on the trees
Warmth of the sun encouraging the bees.

But what of the things that cannot be seen?
A duck, nesting quietly on eggs, so serene.
Or the cancer surreptitiously concealed
Will the diagnosis be repealed?

No repealing, face reality!
Trust for now in the surgeon's ability.
The growth is removed, in its place just pain
A body that will ne'er be quite the same.

Now it's healing, recovery and hope
Be optimistic, don't sit and mope.
Enjoy those "Get Well" cards and flowers
And visitors who sit and talk for hours!

For this time of inertia, I thank God
Though doing 'nothing' to me feels quite odd.
Time to pray, to think and to question
Seeking understanding and direction.

A time to accept my own mortality,
A wake up call, finally reality.
So lonely; for spiritual help I crave
Fear, uncertainty, ere reaching the grave.

Has the cancer gone? We do not know.
More treatment needed, that comes as a blow.
Chemotherapy, that sounds so scary!
And I'm sure that's when one gets less hairy!

Come now and sit in the allotted chair.
There's a clinical smell pervading the air.
A dread in this body that none can see
Are all those syringes really for me?

The dread and the treatment make me so ill,
Must I continue? I don't have the will.
I see the pain in the eyes of my son,
Continue I must 'til the battle's won.

A year has passed, another spring to share.
New life, new hope, yes, and answered prayer.
To say "Thank you" to you who showed such love.
May blessings descend on you from above.

The Pot of Yogurt

Here I stand sedate in a sterile pot,
So carefully made from pasteurised milk.
Gently heated, not too cool or too hot,
Whisked until creamy and textured like silk.

I stand on a shelf now, upright and proud,
With a smart label; eye catching and bright.
Then a smart man, who sticks out from the crowd,
Plucks me away, giving me such a fright!

I'm handled and pinged, put in a bag
Finding I'm sharing with butter and ham!
Where am I going? My hopes quickly sag,
As I'm jolted along; what is the plan?

Phew, that's better! In a cool fridge I'm sat.
I will view the other products here,
There might be some with whom I can chat
Hello, there are eggs and an odd can of beer.

The morning hath come; the fridge door swings wide,
I'm gently removed and put to one side,
To enhance the taste of muesli! I cried!
What! Do you think a yogurt hath no pride?

But I have no choice as I'm ladled out
Onto bits of chopped nuts, fruit and some oat,
I'm brought low; it's obvious I've no clout.
Just wait for this mouthful to reach his throat!

I've been forgotten, left out in the warm,
I should be in the fridge just keeping cool.
Condensation on my pot, I should warn,
Will make me slip and slide, leaving a pool!

That's right, pick me up and put me away
Oh look what you've done! I'm such a disgrace
You've dropped me, what a mess, what can I say?
Spilled from my pot; I'm all over the place!

You have no idea how far I can spread,
Into places you hardly knew existed.
Whatever you touch, wherever you tread,
There is part of me, fully enlisted!

Now the big clean up, find every spore,
Dig out the crack in the posh wood floor!
Don't miss the front of the cabinet door.
And those naughty words I will just ignore!
Spare me a thought, though you're feeling quite raw,
I am no longer a yogurt; I am no more!

HANDS

They ache and throb, grow stiff and cold
Alas, my poor hands are getting old!
Gone are the days of dexterity.
A lesson perhaps in brevity?

The fingers are gnarled and twisted.
No wonder, I'm now ham fisted!
To press, turn, grip or screw, No hope!
Simple tasks now beyond my scope.

As I point west, my finger says east!
That's very confusing to say the least!
The letters I press when I send a text
Leave family and friends completely vexed!

Now it's distortion, lack of activity
Where once, these hands full of creativity,
Would paint and weave, knit and sew
Make exquisite meals, cakes and dough.

Tend the sick, stroke the fevered brow
But alas, only pain and frustration now.
Don't lose hope; they have much yet to give,
And give they will as long as I live.

These hands still reach out in love to touch
Those who are hurting and suffer much.
These hands reassure you are not alone,
I can speak to you as I hold the phone.

These hands I can still manage to raise
Towards my God in worship and praise.
Thanking Him for such beauty to see
Mountain and plain, flowers and tree.

These hands come together in prayer for you
Asking God to bless all the things you do.
Thanking Him for the gift of a friend
Someone so special, on whom to depend,

The Unwanted Marrow!

I started my life as an eager seed
Put in the soil in the hope that I'd breed.
The soil was comfortable, damp and warm
Gradually I felt that I'd been born.

I was tenderly nurtured day by day
Sprinkled with water, caught the sun's bright ray.
Gently danced as the breeze lifted my leaves
Smiled at the visits from the passing bees.

As time went by I burst into flower
Bright yellow, so pretty, not a bit dour!
The bees sang a sweet song on their brief stay
Collecting my nectar to take away.

I'm growing so big now, straining my stalk
Into a growth that will make people gawk!
Each day I drink the sweet water given
Enriched with hormones, subtlety hidden.

Wow! I'm a marrow, just look at my skin
Mottled, green and yellow, shiny and thin.
Inside my skin is succulent white flesh
Pick me now whilst I am perfectly fresh.

I am so versatile, cook me with beans
A delicious, exquisite dish for queens.
You can stuff me, or make a marrow cake
I can be gently boiled or slowly baked.

Alas, when harvested, me and my mates
Are just unwanted on so many plates
All I can say on behalf of all marrow
Open your minds and stop being narrow!

Being unwanted is hurtful you know
But us marrows will continue to grow
For those with taste and a certain finesse
We will grow fat and give of our best!

16

The Great Nine O!

This is written for my dearest friend Jo
On aspiring to reach the great 'nine o'.
Each birthday is special, as you well know,
Marking each step through life as you go.

It is a privilege and a great joy
To bring salutations. Oh don't be coy!
No inhibitions, just simply enjoy
All the cards and presents your friends deploy.

For someone who's attained this great milestone
Should be held in great esteem, please don't groan!
Should be spoilt with cake and perhaps a scone
And sung 'Happy Birthday' in dulcet tone.

Just one point, an observation I make
When you reach nine o some precautions take.
Slow down a little and for goodness sake,
Don't take up rock climbing or learn to skate!

Now all that is left for me to say
Is, I hope you have a memorable day,
That every moment and in every way
You are blessed; for that is how I will pray.

CANADA

Ah Canada, for many years a dream,
A reality now it would seem!
A country of beauty and splendour
Of grandeur, but yet remains tender.
Mountains so vast, putting man in his place
Rivers and streams flow in rapid grace,
Glaciers striving, groaning as they shrink
Giving the water falls something to drink!

A place where the black and grizzly bear roam
Where chipmunk, moose and elk feel at home;
Where eagle, osprey and owl fly free.
A country that has welcomed you and me.
A country that has made a dream come true;
Myriads of 'photos to take home to view!
We have seen the mighty Niagara Falls
An awesome sight that totally enthrals.

We've dined in style at the C.N. Tower
Slowly revolving by unseen power;
Seeing the views of Toronto below
And savoured salmon from the river flow.
We've traversed across the country by train
Letting the Canadian rail take the strain!
Through forests of trees, the aspen and pine
Watching them pass, as we lavishly dine.

Then snowflakes fall, turning green to white
A Christmas card scene, in May, what delight!
Mighty rivers, thunderous falls go by
As rocky mountains reach up to the sky.
It's onto the coach as we leave the train,
Reaching Jasper, as the sun starts to wane;
A quaint little town, where elk like to meet
Away from the wolves, on their nightly beat.

Onwards we go, all eyes for wild life pealed
An animal spied, we are all so thrilled!
It's Banff National Park for a few days stay

A trip in the Gondola on the way,
Up Sulphur Mountain, to reach rocky heights
Even more breathtaking, inspiring sights!

Tis the Rockie Mountaineer! All aboard!
Keep a look out for eagles white and bald,
And goats that balance on the mountain sides.
Past rivers, through tunnels this great train glides.
Then without warning the tundra changes
Goodbye to those snow-capped mountain ranges.

This desert has a beauty of its own
No rainfall here, 'tis as dry as a bone!
But as the sun strikes these rocks, it shows clear
Metallic colours, in tier after tier.
The meerkat pops his head out from the rock,
Is that surprise on his face? Or mere shock?

This has been a story that must be told
We booked a trip in silver, but got gold!
In a domed carriage, clear views all around
We were pampered, spoilt, as Vancouver bound.
Delicious meals, served to us in our seats
To be sure we didn't miss any treats.

We have reached Vancouver, still more to see
As the coach wends its way, ere home for tea.
Rivers and bridges; large gardens, lush green;
The only clock in the world, powered by steam.
Small river buses nipping here and there
Sky scrapers with their noses in the air!

Yet to come; still more adventures and views
As aboard the Volendam for a cruise.
It's "life boat drill" so we know what to do!
No time to unpack or seek out a loo!
Gradually finding our way aboard ship
As quietly she lets her mooring ropes slip.

Out on the deck as we steam through the sea
Leaving behind us a wash as we flee.

Eyes peeled watching for creatures rarely seen,
Porpoises, whales, pointing out where they've been!
The sea-lions and seals are easier to spot
As are the eagles soaring way o're the top.

Sailed into ports to places with strange names
Hustle and bustle of boats and sea planes.
Janeau and Skagway of Gold Rush renown,
Walking the broad walks; taking in the town.
To colourful Ketchikan, known world wide
For delicious salmon, pure red not dyed!

Words I find fail me for this special day,
The spectacular cruise of Glacier Bay.
Rugged landscape rising to rocky peaks
Awesome glaciers; hark, as nature speaks.
Icebergs floating on the sea of azure
Reflecting the sky in resplendence pure.

The trip is over, yet will ever be
Something so special in the heart of me.
For friends we made, for the moments of pleasure
So many things to store and treasure.
No longer a dream, but a dream come true.
Should I dream again? Should the dream be new?

A Mechanically Useful Machine: MUM, The Robot

Come meet my mum, she's just like a robot
She knows just who, why, where and what!
No matter what you ask, she has a solution
And carries out chores with precise execution.

When day begins there is a call
Breakfast is ready, it's time for school.
She has life's solutions at her finger tips
Like, "where's me shirt" or "I feel sick!"

She sees us safely on our way
Then it's into overdrive, for the rest of the day!
She goes to work or stays at home
You never really hear her moan!

She does the washing, hoovers the floor
Ironing, baking, shopping and more.
There's no end to the things she does in a day,
And fancy, she does it for love and not pay!

Home from school. Such hard work we've done!
What's for tea? We are starving Mum.
On the floor we hang our coats and bags
For whoever heard of a robot who nags?

Now tea is over, we've had our fill.
We'll watch some telly; I think it's The Bill.
But along comes that robot, no time to shirk
Turn off that telly and do your homework.

We are off to bed, it's night time now
Mum Robot can reduce her power.
But on tick over she must remain
In case we wake at night in pain!

But what we would really like to say
To all our mums who are here today,
A great big "thank you" for all you do.
We love you, and wouldn't change one of you!

A Poem for Christmas

Christmas is coming, how can you tell?
It's mid November, hear the shops' gentle knell
Persistently saying "come ye faithful and spend,
You know you can use your flexible friend!"

But time rushes past and before you know
We're in the grip of winter, a sprinkling of snow.
Christmas! Good gracious, is that the date?
I've done it again, I'm behind, I'm late!

It's off to town, no time to stop,
I'll buy my cards from the charity shop.
Now what to buy Father? He's always a pain
If I get him more socks, he's bound to complain.

Being bustled about from left to right
No time to look at the twinkling lights.
As "Silent Night" blares out from the tannoy.
Is this what they mean by peace and joy?

Now it's off to the supermarket, no time to spare
For I've got to buy the Christmas fare.
I struggle down each aisle, without a moan
Pushing a trolley that has a will of its own!

With trolley full, the shopping complete,
I know we've got more than enough to eat.
Time is getting short, there's still much to do
And I'm sure I'm stood in the slowest queue!

I'm beginning to get the festive feel
It's either that or I'm getting a chill.
As Christmas greetings drop upon the mat
Whoops! That's another I've forgotten – drat!

It's Christmas Eve and I'm well puffed
The turkey's sat there, not yet … ready!
The Christmas tree lights have gone on the blink.
Where's the spare bulb? I forgot it, I think.

I've done the sprouts, the presents are wrapped
Now I'm exhausted, my energy sapped.
Do you think next year that I will remember?
To get ready for Christmas in mid November?

I cannot help feeling we've moved far away
From that dirty old stable, and the first Christmas Day.
A moment, a thought, about a dear Saviour's birth,
God's gift of love, for each person on earth.

The Donkey

I am a donkey, grey with long ears
I've done lots of things over the years
I've walked many miles, bearing the loads
Traversed through desert, walked country roads.

You may think this donkey, grey with long ears
Like any old donkey; no worries or fears.
But I'm very special, yet humble
You never hear me complain or grumble.

This special donkey, grey with long ears
Is to take a long journey, so it appears
To Bethlehem, so my master doth say
When we arrive, we'll need somewhere to stay.

Sat on this donkey, grey with long ears
Is Mary, Joseph's fiancée, one hears.
She's expecting a baby, I must take care
Not to stumble or fall, of bandits beware.

Such noise that greets donkey, grey with long ears
Masses of people, soldiers with spears
No room to stay and we badly need rest
Won't anyone welcome us as their guest?

An inn keeper leads donkey, grey with long ears
Round to a stable, no comfort he fears.
It is warm and dry with plenty of hay
This will do nicely, we gratefully say.

What a night for donkey, grey with long ears!
Angels are singing, bringing good cheers
Smelly shepherds, come in with their sheep
And there in my manger a baby doth sleep!

A dream thought this donkey, grey with long ears
A wondrous sight as he wipes away tears
"Look!" said the cow as he nudged my rib
"That's God's precious Son, lying in that crib."

Now life for this donkey, grey with long ears
Will ne'er be the same for his remaining years
A witness to those great events of old
To the greatest story ever told.

The Supermarket

All tills in the store go beep beep; beep beep.
The poor cashiers must hear it in their sleep!
Each product that passes must go beep beep
Whether it be costly or whether cheap!

Enter the store to the music beep beep
Up and down aisles searching out food to keep.
Filling the trolley with items to beep
Doing the shopping in one fair sweep.

Queue up at the till, unload this great heap
On the conveyer belt the products creep
Item follows item as if they were sheep
But instead of bleating, they go beep beep!

Mr Tesco, Morrison, Asda do greet
The sound of the till as it goes beep beep.
Mr Sainsbury, Waitrose, Spar don't sleep
Unless they can hear a constant beep beep!

Teeth

I never thought the day would come
And it makes me feel pretty glum
To admit I have less teeth than gum
This really isn't any fun

Oh, dentist, what's the cause of this?
I've brushed and rinsed without a miss
I've kept away from drinks that fizz
Not eaten sweets that pop and whizz.

Booze I've kept to the minimum
Steering clear of the gin and rum.
Fruit and veggie to fill my tum.
Now a plate with false teeth to come!

Sit in my chair, and open wide,
Just a small plate will be required
Said my dentist with dental pride.
As my mouth smiled and I just sighed!

The plate is in, I chomp away
My words spoken with a gentle spray!
My gums tolerate them day by day
My heart is broke as I now pay!

Vision

What a wonderful place, familiar, yet totally new.
Swathes of green; emerald mossy banks, sparkling morning dew.
Flowers blooming brightly, in orange, yellow, crimson and blue,
Leafy trees with their branches dripping with fruits of tender hue.

Birds, whose harmony fills the air with the sweetest of song,
Heard above the trickle of the stream that gently flows along.
In the distance the rushing of water as it falls headlong
Over the precipice, its abrupt descent, forceful and strong.

A feeling of warmth surrounds me, people are gentle and kind.
Smiling, inviting, befriending, wanting to give of their time.
I want to walk and talk with them. Please, do not leave me behind!
I'm tired of being a scapegoat, taking blame, time after time.

In the city here the pavements glitter, children laugh and play,
Ethereal beings enjoy the splendour of gems on display,
Gates of pearl, crystal lakes, angels with their wings that swish and sway.
Across the sky a rainbow makes a canopy o'er the day.

There's a throne room, brilliant gold, where a king reigns over all
Holds justice in his hand, yet his eyes of softest brown, enthral.
His inherent gift is love as he keeps his absolute rule
He knows me by name, enjoys me near, I love to hear his call.

Because the rule is just and fair, it's a tranquil place to dwell
As I look around at the beauty, my heart begins to swell
There is no place on earth that compares or yet one can foretell.
For it is a vision I hold dear, not let time ever quell.

Hinterland

In this remote Hinterland, it is cold, oh, so cold!
A great expanse of hoar frost, no sun with rays of gold.
Trees without leaves stand like skeletons, all grandeur gone.
No blade of grass grows, no colour, no laughter, no song!
Tis a place of great sorrow, where people don't belong
But alas, day by day, year by year the people throng.

The sweet song of the bird unheard in this barren waste
The sound of the bee, the call of the wild, not a trace!
No sound of rushing water, crystal lakes now solid ice.
Any new hope that might have surfaced is gone in a trice.
I look at passing faces of the citizens here
Expressions cold and frozen, no hint of any cheer.

I try to exchange greetings, but just get a frozen stare
There is no warmth of companionship, no friendly air!
I look into their eyes, yes, I see such deep despair.
Love and hope is missing here, but does anyone care?
How did they come to be here? Surely not aware
Perhaps it is a warning for all, let us then beware!

A Selection of Vegetables!

Carrot or stick, Carrot or stick
Come on now and take your pick.
Crunchy and sweet if eaten raw
Good for exercising the jaw!
Bite me and get an orange spark
Wow, you can now see in the dark!

There are French and English, yellow and green
Red and white can also be seen.
Pungent taste; vitamin C and B six
They add life to any dish you might fix.
Although they might bring a tear to your eyes
Knowing your onions is to be quite wise!

Consider the humble sprout
Much maligned without a doubt.
Round and firm and very green
Petal leaves with perfect sheen.
A traditional Christmas fayre;
Later, you really must beware
As they slowly digest within
They can give you awful wind!

I love to grow potatoes
'Cause you never really knows
When you thrust your fork into the ground
How many potatoes will be found.
You take your seed potatoes
Let them chit before you sow.

Then quickly pop them in the ground
Comfy in a firm and earthy mound.
Then let nature do her very best
Pray you avoid the potato pest.
Then hey! The day of harvest comes
Potatoes, potatoes by the tons!

A Holiday to Remember!

A holiday to remember, I should say,
Excursions and trips every day.
Around Lake Garda with views superb
Through villages of names we'd never heard.
In and out of tunnels, round hair-pin bends
Sitting, chatting and making new friends.
But, as Laura was chatting, dumb she was struck
As we came face to face with a mighty big truck.
An impasse, as neither could move
The skills of the driver, now we will prove!
After forty five minutes of gesticulation,
Edging and creeping, deep concentration.
Eventually released like a bat out of hell
We continue our journey, with more tales to tell!

We journeyed to Venice and also Verona
With Pino sending my friend in a coma.
Now Pino was our guide extraordinaire
With his yellow umbrella held high in the air.
In Venice we followed his instructions clear
Not to get lost, or be late. But be back here!
To the Rialto Bridge we made our way
With a pizza in hand, keeping hunger at bay.
Aboard the boat, a trip on the Lagoon,
Then our day in Venice over, all too soon.

Up to the Dolomites to reach nine thousand feet,
Twisting and turning, it was ever so steep!
The wind did blow and the air was cold
As we boarded the gondola, ever so bold.
Fantastic! Mountain peaks covered with snow
Guess who played snowballs? I don't know!

We'd return to the Drago at the end of each day
To get ready for dinner without too much delay.
The food was so good, the company was great
We chatted and laughed as we emptied our plate.
But as the only Sassenach on a table of four
I learnt more about Scots, than I knew before!

They were very gracious and soon they forgot
I was English, but made an associate Scot.

Off to ones room at the end of the day.
A last look at the lake as the light fades away.
I stand on the balcony, has Romeo come hither?
Alas 'tis only the dragon in the garden thither.
And so to bed with more memories to store
Of another memorable holiday, to be sure.

A Special Gift

God gave me a gift some years ago,
That gift was friendship; I'd like you to know,
God knew how much I needed a friend;
Someone trustworthy on whom to depend.

My friend and I know each other well!
Spoken of things, only a friend you can tell.
We have shared joy and pain, laughter and tears,
Much good news, some bad over the years.

But holidays together are special indeed,
When the time comes, we are off with all speed;
And we've heard it said, and often recall,
Some people would like to be a fly on the wall!

We forget our ages when we've said our goodbyes,
And enjoy this time to act out our shoe size!
Great fun has been had, much laughter too,
Chuckle muscles exercised through and through.

One of our holidays was a silent retreat.
We failed abysmally in this difficult feat.
We'd come down for meals, chat, chatting away,
Then hear a great Shhhh… be silent, I pray!

We have played in the snow on the Dolomites,
We have visited Norway with its fantastic sights,
Enjoyed rounds of putting with conkers for balls.
Stood on the mountains watching great water falls.

My friend once taught me to play croquet
She had two sets of rules, and I have to say,
Mine were to lose and hers to win!
Though, I still regret when the ball hit her shin!

We often got lost when going somewhere,
Road signs and arrows just shouldn't be there!
They point us in ways we don't want to go
My friend just ignores them; we don't go with the flow!

Sometimes my friend gets peeved with me
Like saying "buy one get one free"!
In reply to a guest who was rather posh
Who said "you've identical coats" Oh gosh!

I don't want to die, so I won't go on!
I don't want to bore you, as time has gone.
But I'd like you to know, I thank God each day
For a gift so precious, given me that day.

But before I sign off, I almost forgot
To tell you I am an Associate Scot!
Although a Sassenach, I can boast
To be part of a country my friend loves most.

As for my friend, a stalwart is she
Imagine how life without her would be!
Without her! I question; for her promise to me,
Is she'll come back and haunt me, frequently!

The Motorway Coffee

We left home with expectations,
Hailed the coach with salutations
Off on a day trip. What a lark!
Our visit today is Bletchley Park.

Into the coach, grab a front seat!
Stow coats and baggage, food to eat.
To fellow travellers, nod "hello"
Safety belts on, then off we go.

We don't move far, we're in a jam!
The road ahead blocked with car and van.
It takes a lot to practise grace
We crawl along at a snail's pace.

Our journey time is all to cock!
But we really do need to stop
The morning cuppa has passed through,
Most are desperate for the loo!

Motorway services at last
We leave the coach thick and fast
Relieved and comfortable once more.
Ah, refreshments now, through this door.

We'll have some coffee to cheer us up
Small, medium, large size of cup
Its Costa, and it Costa a lot
For that I could have bought the pot!

What is worse, the coffee is foul!
Enough to make a person yowl
What should have been a welcome break,
Don't choose Costa your thirst to slake!

The School Nativity

The children line up and excitement spills,
The shepherds are out on the makeshift hills
With their sheep, although confused, staying close by.
O'er the stable a bright star in the sky.

Mary and Joseph arrive on the scene
Mary turns, waves to her Mum she's just seen!
A tug from Joseph, she's back in the play
They trudge along seeking a place to stay.

The inn keeper tells them to go away!
No! No! Teacher signals; ask them to stay.
The inn keeper huffs, and lets them come in
Not hiding his feelings full of chagrin.

In the stable baby Jesus is born
With donkey and cow looking quite forlorn.
Angels appear! Scare the shepherds and sheep,
Well after all, they were fast asleep!

Angels are singing with their wings spread wide
Gabriel's halo has slipped to one side.
One of the sheep has decided to flee
He is off to the loo to have a wee!

The kings enter in wearing regal crowns
Dressed in magnificent bright coloured gowns.
As they kneel in homage, slightly adrift
They reluctantly hand over their gifts!

A gallant performance can't be denied
As parents and friends applaud with great pride.
Forget the tinsel and decking the hall
This nativity expresses it all!

A Winter's Morning

'Tis a lovely morning though very cold
Sparkling frost, touched by a rising sun's gold
Great oaks reach up into inky blue sky
Not dressed in their leaves, sculptured, stretch high.

Time to don boots and to wrap up warm
A privilege indeed to greet the dawn.
The fallen leaves crunch underneath one's feet
An air of expectation of whom I'll meet.

Across the fields rabbits run to and fro
Standing very still, a stag with his doe
In the distance a fox seems to glide along
This all done to the sweet sound of bird song.

The frost has highlighted the spider's web
Beautiful patterns of delicate thread
No sign of the spider, he's hidden away.
But from afar I hear a horse's neigh.

Trudging onwards, I see Storm and Ryan
Patiently waiting for their morning bran
Their ears prick up as I enter their field
In my pocket fresh carrot chopped and peeled!

Time to ponder and to evaluate
As I cross the field, climb the five bar gate.
Speak to Fee tucked up in her warm stable
Eating the hay hanging down from the gable.

Home to the warmth and work of the day
A walk in the morning, a wonderful way
To reflect and respond to nature's delights
Before facing the day's various plights!

I wish I'd said "NO"

Christmas is over, how I wish I'd said "no"
To the biscuits and sweets, the wine that did flow.
Do not mention mince pies. Or that knob of cream!
No wonder my clothes are straining at the seam!

If I'd only said "no" to the Christmas cake
To those nuts and raisins, the chocolate flake
Chocolate Roses that "grow on you" 'tis true
As my waistband refuses to stretch anew.

I could have said "no", so I shouldn't bleat
As I munched my way through the Quality Street,
Christmas pudding with brandy butter and cream
Now look at the size of my receding beam!

I would have said "no" had they not been proffered
But alas, such little will power I offered.
So now the new year diet will kick in
Until I've lost weight and down to one chin!

The Fisherman

He sits on the bank, with rod in his hand
Hope against hope he'd bring something to land.
Under the water, "not us," said the fish,
"We'll swim away, not give him his wish!"

He sits on the bank, wrapped up nice and warm
A solitary figure, quite forlorn.
Dreaming of catching a bream, chub or carp
As hour passes hour, until it's quite dark!

He sits on the bank, on his fishing seat
A selection of bait for the fish to eat.
He takes his rod and attaches his line
And selects a hook that's without a spine.

He sits on the bank and scratches his brow
With what shall he tempt those fishes with now?
Wriggling maggots or a juicy fat worm?
Whatever! He'll sit and enjoy his sojourn.

He sits on the bank, his eyes slowly close
He says he is thinking, not in a doze!
As time slips by, will a fish ever bite?
Alas it appears not a fish in sight.

He sits on the bank as day turns to night.
Shocked back to life as a fish takes a bite!
It splashes and pulls, making a great play
Wow! It's a tiddler, the catch of the day!

Shopping!

It's that time of year again; Christmas is coming
Off to town, though it's cold and finger numbing.
Entering the arcade full of amazing shops
Looking for inspiration, no doodling, don't stop!

Once in Royal David's City, in the background
Shoppers chat, their thoughts elsewhere, hardly hear the sound.
The card machines, swallowing numbers, pin after pin
If they had facial features, they'd wear a huge grin!

Finding inspiration, I'm now weighed down with bags
Home now to unpack and remove the price tags!
A strong cup of tea and a sigh of relief,
That's Christmas shopping done without too much grief!

Deary me, Dad's gloves don't fit, back to town I go
Hop on the bus without any fuss, oh so slow.
Grid locked roads, traffic heading to town for the sales
Start, stop, start, all eager to seek the bargain grails.

Off the bus into the shop, people everywhere
Pushing and shoving, chase after their chosen fayre.
Are these the same shoppers who, a few days ago,
Were chatting and smiling with their faces aglow?

No, no, it can't be, that such a simple word, "sale"
Should turn a person wild, it is beyond the pale!
But it's true; I have witnessed it with my own eye
The word "sale" turns a person into Jekyll and Hyde!

Whoops!

A new day is dawning
A beautiful morning
It's crisp and dry and white
As Jack Frost sparkles bright.

Then all of a sudden
As if by a bludgeon
I am prone on the ground
Felled without any sound.

I was down in a trice
As my foot met black ice
But the first thing I quell
Is a loud painful yell!

Make sure I am alone
Before giving a groan
Can't risk one's dignity
Or show timidity!

Alone, no prying eyes
To laugh at my demise
I get up from the ground
No broken bones are found!

The moral of this tale
Ignore wind, rain and hail.
But be aware of ice
Before you tread, think twice!

Are You ready for Christmas?

Tis Christmas time, Tis Christmas time
Once more I pen a little rhyme
I hope to raise a smile or two
But there is a question I ask of you.

Are you ready for Christmas?

I'll start early this year to avoid the crush
I'll select my presents without undue rush.
Mince pies and cake will be baked in good time
Then I can smugly say, "I've done all of mine!"

But you know how it is, time rushes on
You thought you had weeks, but somehow they've gone
Not a present, a card or a decoration
Those good intentions turn to desperation.

So it's off to town to join the throng
Setting off with a cheery "I shan't be long!"
A shirt for him and of course some socks
And a book on the latest boats and yachts.

My feet are aching, my head is a throb
What can I buy Father? It is a job!
A gardening voucher, that's just the ticket
He can buy some seeds or spring onions with it.

It gets worse of course as the day draws near
I'm sick of hearing about Christmas cheer!
A visit to the supermarket I've yet to make
And that's enough to make anyone quake!

Into the supermarket with an audible groan,
I've picked the trolley with a will of its own!
Up and down aisles, Ah, the end is in view
And now I'm stood in the slowest queue!

The Christmas tree has pride of place
The fairy's not happy by the look on her face!

The tree looks lovely, but I stand aghast
As the blinking lights have blinked their last!

I'm wrapping presents, such awkward shapes!
And I keep losing the end of the sellotape.
The decorations are up, let's hope they stay
And don't fall down on Christmas Day!

As the carol says, "All is calm, all is bright,"
Let's ponder now on this Christmas Eve night.
Are you ready for Christmas, I ask again?
Or is it just trappings and tinsel, all vain?

The Garden Shed

I seldom go down to the garden shed,
On the times I do, it fills me with dread!
Because that shed holds a lifetime's hoard
When I look in, I could fall on my sword!

It's my husband's retreat, you'll find him inside
Hidden away in his personal hide.
Soothing music plays on the radio
Door firmly shut holding the status quo!

This shed is full of gadgets and machines
A locomotive built, powered by steam
Each casting shaped, milled and drilled to the plans
The lathe turning under capable hands.

There are nuts and bolts, nails and screws galore
Hammers and chisels, files you can't ignore,
Saws of all sizes with variant speed
A big box of scrap, he's sure he might need!

It's a comfy shed, with plenty of light
A pot belly stove burning warm and bright,
With wood and nuggets to keep it alight
I wonder at times if he's there for the night!

No place for a garden fork, spade or hoe,
No room for shears, rake or machine to mow.
No empty pots for the mouse to make home
No spiders welcome or even a drone.

We have to accept that the garden shed
Has changed its allegiance and is instead,
A man's bolthole where he can ferret away
Keeping out of sight and the Mrs at bay!

My New Fleeced Lined Tights

I went down to church the other day
I thought 'twould be nice to go and pray.
The organist played, the choir did sing
The elastic in my tights went ping!

I stood up to sing, sat down to pray
Alas my tights did not obey!
I tried an inconspicuous hitch,
Perhaps it would appear I had an itch.

My concentration was at an ebb
As my tights were creeping down the leg!
Hope upon hope the service would end
So then I could quickly homeward wend.

We said Amen, I gave one great hitch
I should get away without a glitch!
Away down the path through the cemetery
As my tights made it down to the knee!

The Spider

I don't like spiders, they give me the creeps
Eight legged creatures seem never to sleep
They run fast across floors and up the wall
They can hang upside down and never fall.

They climb up the plughole into the bath
Hide in the overflow having a laugh!
Unlike a mouse who runs away in fear
The spider stalks towards you wearing a sneer.

He moves in silence, not a sound doth stray,
He seeks out victims to become his prey.
If you looked into his eyes, cold and black,
You would know at once that you're his next snack!

He spins his web like a bicycle wheel
A work of art; attracting prey to kill.
Wrapping his prey with silk spun fine,
In go the fangs then the poison like wine!

What do I do when this creature I face?
I grab the hoover, with the hose I make chase.
With suction on full, he won't get away
Down the hosepipe, that's the end of his day!

Mother's Day

Dear Mum, it is your special day
So I took up my pen, these words to say
How much I appreciate the things you do
I will be more specific, just for you.

I'm sure you know what's best for me
And I'm sorry at times we just don't agree!
When I'm feeling wide awake
It's off to bed for goodness sake;
Then in the morning when sleep is divine
It's wakey, wakey rise and shine!

After eating your breakfast, that's never a hit
It's off to school, when I'm sure I'm not fit.
But when I come home, it's your smile I see
Or could it be a grimace? Maybe!
I know you have been through my bedroom door
And seen my clothes hung upon the floor
Or maybe it's the rubbish on the bed
And you're worried where I'll lay my head!

Being a mother isn't easy I bet
You can tell when I shower, without getting wet!
You know when the toothpaste misses the brush
And when I've done wrong, by the way I blush.
I tease the dog and pull his tail
And forget my chores without fail!

So to you, my mum, on this your special day
Thank you as you guide me along life's way
Imagine you the oyster, me the grain of sand,
One day I'll be a pearl within your hand!
The oyster must have her irritations
Of these I have no limitations!

My Brother

He was just sixteen and a day
When his life was taken away.
A lorry struck that fatal blow
The pain he felt, we'll never know.

He left behind a heartbroken mother
Father, two sisters and a brother.
The numbness of these early days
Each facing death in different ways.

A life changing event for all
At his young age death shouldn't call.
Family life is now a strain
Each trying not to cause more pain.

Choose flowers; what words will you write?
None, I yell, this just isn't right!
I can't write or say what I think
I'll just make lines with pen and ink.

A service was led for us all
There were rows of boys from the school.
The church was full, the coffin stood
The pastor's words not understood.

An inquest; accidental death,
Does it matter when there is no breath?
For the driver of the lorry
A time to say he is sorry!

We laughed, fought, cycled together
Long walks that went on forever,
Sneaked to the pictures and the fair
Knowing that we shouldn't be there!

You are remembered year by year
Sometimes a smile, sometimes a tear.
As time and life move swiftly on
Still 'tis hard to accept you're gone!

A Touch of Ice

We're off on a trip to the Northern heights,
Excited to see such fantastic sights.
We board a boat that has been tried and tested,
Sailed oceans for fifty years unmolested.
Ensconced in our cabin, baggage stowed
We must explore and capture this other mode!

The language has changed, no back or front now
For the back is called stern, the front called the bow.
Your left becomes port and starboard your right
And you gaze o'er the side from such a great height!

Adventure has started, we nose out to sea
Leaving behind hustle at port and quay.
Time to relax, savour the evening fare,
To meet fellow travellers gathered there.

We plough through the night, get a taste of the sea
As we pitch and roll, reunited with tea!
Stagger for the pills to prevent these ills
Balanced? As yet, have not acquired these skills!

Don hats, coats, gloves and boots up to the knee,
We board the coach, places of interest to see.
Museums with relics of life in the past,
Cathedrals with windows of stunning stained glass.

The Northern Lights, will they appear and dance?
As we drive through the snow blizzard, no chance!
We alight from the coach, stars fill the sky
Come forth, you lights; It's no time to be shy!

Crunchy snow underfoot, glittering knolls
Myriad of stars on deep blue velvet stoles.
Gradually those Northern Lights rise from sleep
Tinged green, slowly dancing, the earth to seek.

Now a wonder rarely seen, The Ice Hotel
Ice sculptures blue, white, keep one under their spell.

For a short season only, then melt away
Back to sparkling water under the sun's ray.

Be the sea rough or calm, 'tis homeward bound
Sailing home to our old familiar ground
With memories of those met, places we've seen
Having fulfilled one of those insatiable dreams!

Toothpaste Dilemma!

I need to renew the toothpaste
I suppose I did it in haste.
I looked at the shelf in despair
At the number of choices there!
One to protect the cavity
Or whiten with intensity
Triple action, or sensitive
Or just everything to brush with!

Pump action sounds good, I'll take that
No middle tube to go flat!
But when I came to brush my teeth
It really was beyond belief.
I pumped and shook to no avail
It really was a sorry tale.
The toothpaste just refused to show
E'en though I danced the Dosey Doe!

Election Colours

O where shall I put my cross this year?
Should I go for blue without a fear?
But what of the red, I've heard what they've said,
Should I ditch the blue, vote red instead?
Then there is orange, a Lib Dem pack
Middle of the road, not white or black!
Now purple would make a pleasant change,
But would my friends think me rather strange?
What about an environmental theme?
Would my pen allow me to cross the green?
A rainbow of colour for any voter,
I think I'll stay a voting floater!

The Missing Padlock

He unlocked the padlock from the gate
Placed it on the top bar, then too late
The gate swung open, the lock took flight
In the blink of an eye, out of sight.
On hands and knees he scrabbled around
But alas the lock could not be found!
He would get his mate to help him look
He came prepared with scythe and a hook.
Cutting through the bramble and nettle
Not a sign of the shining metal!
Then a friend with a detector came,
She searched and fumbled, but all in vain.
But a passer-by looked on the ground
There a shining lock lay safe and sound!

Memories

On a trip to Devon in early May,
We visited Totnes along the way.
From there we would see the steam engine run,
Transporting us back to when we were young!
We'd hang over bridges to see the train pass,
Enveloped in the steam that it blast.
The train had gone leaving in its traces
Sooty black smuts on our clothes and faces!
Puff, puff of the engine, whistle shrill
Even today brings a nostalgic thrill!

The Slug!

It's time to garden. Spring is here
Grass to mow and hedges to shear
Seeds to sow, bedding plants to rear
Veggie patch to dig, weeds to clear.

Dead head the bulbs, they're past their best
So many jobs, no time to rest.
Water and nurture, watch them grow
Little seedlings all in a row.

Then comes the day for planting out,
The plants have grown, they're strong and stout.
Come summer they will look divine,
A radiance of colour sublime.

Catastrophe, no plant in sight!
Disappeared, all in one night.
Not the minutest sign of a plug
Eaten, demolished by the slug!